Rocky
and the
Lamb

For my daughter Pepa
G. G.

For Ava
L. C.

First published in Great Britain in 2006 by
Gullane Children's Books
This paperback edition first published in 2007 by

Gullane Children's Books
185 Fleet Street, London EC4A 2HS
www.gullanebooks.com

10   9   8   7   6   5   4   3   2

Text © Greg Gormley 2006
Illustrations © Lynne Chapman 2006

The right of Greg Gormley and Lynne Chapman to be identified as the author and illustrator of
this work has been asserted by them in accordance with the Copyright, Designs and Patents Act, 1988.
A CIP record for this title is available from the British Library.

ISBN: 978-1-86233-675-9

Printed and bound in China

Rocky
and the Lamb

Greg Gormley

illustrated by
Lynne Chapman

GULLANE
CHILDREN'S BOOKS

In a misty, murky, far-flung land, a gloomy mountain stood.
At the mountain's thorny foot, in a lonely stony pass,
behind a boulder, lived a wolf called Rocky.
He was not a noble or a handsome beast.
Mean and cowardly as a dog at bath-time,
Rocky was a horrible bully.

As travellers trudged through the pass, Rocky would steal their valuables, or even their non-valuables. Indeed, Rocky would steal anything at all.

If he met a small animal carrying something nice, he would say, **"Hey Shorty, hand it over,"** in the most menacing way possible.

But if a large creature travelled by,
no matter how tempting
their belongings looked,
the wolf would hide behind
his rock and let them pass.

One day Rocky spied a sweet little lamb picking its way along the path. It was carrying a small, plain box.

"How nice," said Rocky to himself.
"A present for me."

As the lamb drew closer, the wolf sprang out.
"Hey, marshmallow-face,"
he snarled. **"What's in the box?"**

"A splendid crown for the king's birthday," said the lamb,
who was polite and shy but not at all afraid. "It is guarded by
the scariest, hairiest monster you could possibly imagine."

"Oh, well, the palace is, erm . . . that way,"
lied Rocky, pointing to a little mountain path.
I'll find a way to get that splendid crown, he thought.

The path wound upwards, and up and up again,
towards the very peak of the mountain. Delicately the
lamb tippy-toed in and out of the scratching, scraping
thorn bushes that covered the mountainside.

"Ee, ow, ouch!" cried Rocky
as he tried to follow.

PALACE

Next the lamb skipped in and out of the crashing, bashing rocks.

Bink,

bonk,

donk!

bounced the rocks and stones
off poor Rocky's head.

PALACE THIS WAY

Finally the lamb stepped lightly over deep mounds of snow.

"Brrr," shivered Rocky
as he landed in the middle of a snowdrift.

Meanwhile the lamb had reached
the top of the mountain and the end of the path.
Finding no palace, she shrugged her shoulders and sat down.

Carefully she opened the magic box and . . .

took out her lunch
of fresh bread, a handsome green apple
and a jug of creamy milk to drink.

There was indeed a most splendid crown,
which she placed on a small satin cushion,
but no sign at all of a monster.

Pah! There never was a monster, thought Rocky,
I'm having that crown.
But by the time he had struggled free of the snow,
the lamb had already set off on her way again.

The lamb trod softly over the freezing snow.
Rocky waded after her, spluttering and shuddering —
he was so **c-c-cold** and **wet**.

With a hop, skip and a dainty pirouette, the lamb passed each falling rock untouched. But every lump seemed to clobber Rocky no matter how he dodged and weaved.

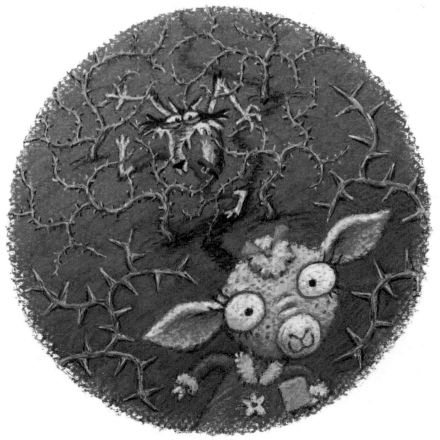

Between those terrible thorns the lamb slipped completely unscathed, but every single spike seemed to snag and tear at Rocky until he was so tender that he yelped. But the lamb didn't hear a thing, and she skipped along quite merrily.

At last Rocky caught up with the lamb.
"Oh, Mr Wolf, I got lost! How good of you to
come and help me," said the lamb, happy to see him.
**"I'll help you in a minute.
Now give me that box**,"
growled the wolf.

Rocky snatched the
box and lifted the lid.
"Mr Wolf, wait—" began the
lamb, but it was too late . . .

Out of the box flew the **scariest, hairiest monster** you could possibly imagine!

The monster chased Rocky through the
scratching, scraping thorns. "**Ow!**"

The monster chased Rocky through the
crashing, bashing rocks. **Donk**!

The monster chased Rocky through the
f-f-freezing deep snow. "**Brrr!**"

The monster chased Rocky up and down
and round and round the mountains.

Finally, cornered behind his very own boulder,
Rocky whimpered,
"Please don't get me, scary monster,
I promise I'll be a good wolf."
At that moment the lamb appeared . . .

"I'm so sorry," she said to Rocky.
"Leave Mr Wolf alone, you naughty monster!
He was only trying to help me get to the palace."
The monster slunk back into the box
looking a little ashamed.

Having apologised again and thanked Rocky for his kindness,
the lamb continued on to the palace
where she told everyone about the nice Mr Wolf.

As for Rocky, he was so sorry for his wickedness,
not to mention his bruises, that he kept his
promise and became a good wolf.

So many of the creatures who had talked to the lamb
asked for his help when passing through the mountains,
that Rocky became a famous mountain guide
and never robbed anyone ever again.

The End